First published in Great Britain in 2007
by Zero To Ten Limited
7A Portman Mansions, Chiltern Street,
London W1U 6NR

This edition © 2007 zero to ten Limited
© Gallimard Jeunesse 2006

First published in France in 2006 as
Rita et Machin à l'école

British Library Cataloguing in Publication Data
Arrou-Vignod, Jean-Philippe, 1958-
Rita and Whatsit at school
1. Rita (Fictitious character : Arrou-Vignod) - Juvenile
fiction 2. Whatsit (Fictitious character) - Juvenile
fiction 3. Schools - Juvenile fiction 4. Children's stories
I. Title
843.9'2[J]

ISBN 9781840895216

Printed in China

JEAN-PHILIPPE ARROU-VIGNOD ✳ OLIVIER TALLEC

Rita and Whatsit at School

ZERO TO TEN

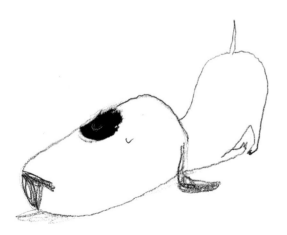

The teacher said no one was allowed to
take soft toys to school.
'Hmm,' thinks Rita.

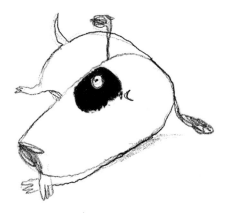

'Well,' says Rita, 'you are not a toy,
you are a real dog. I've got an idea…'

When Rita gets to school the next morning, no
one notices anything odd.
Her friends don't spot anything, and nor does
the teacher.
'No fidgeting,' Rita whispers.
'And hide your nose, or the game is up!'

It's very dark in Rita's
school bag.
Her break time snack smells
very tasty.
So do her dance shoes, and
those half-chewed sweets.

Whatsit is quite happy to take a
little nap…

In class, it's painting time.
Rita tries hard not to go over the edge.

Suddenly…

'Miss! Someone has messed up
my painting!'

Now it's time for gym.

Rita and her friends go for the record in building the highest human pyramid, when suddenly…

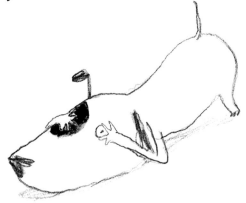

'Miss! Someone pushed me!'

Rita is in the lunch hall.
On the menu are all her favourites –
pasta and peas and peaches.

But suddenly…

'Miss! Someone's pinched food
from my plate!'

'Hello Whatsit. You've
been so good!'

'I've brought you a treat. But
remember – hide your nose!'

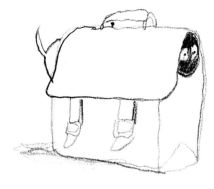

In the classroom, not a sound. Everyone is having a little rest.

Break time!
Rita and her friends build a snowman in
the playground.

'Miss! Someone's hit me
on the head with a snowball!'

'Children!' scolds the teacher.
'You really are impossible today!'

When Rita gets home, all she wants to
do is play with Whatsit.

'Come on, wake up, or I'll call you Limp Rag!'
'Too tired,' yawns Whatsit.

'But you haven't done anything all day,' cries Rita.
'Yes I have, I chewed your shoes…'

'And my half-chewed sweets?'
'I ate those too.'

'Whatsit! That's not allowed!'

Then it is bedtime.
'You know what?' says Rita. 'I've had an idea.
Tomorrow it's swimming at school. What if you
came too? I'll lend you my swimming cap.'

The only answer is a little snore.
Zzzzz.

A first day at school is tiring, even
for a dog with no name!